THIS WOLF HOUND BOOK

BELONGS TO ~

G. Mc Gier

For my sister, Marie,
There are still stories in the lightbulb yet.

BY THE SAME AUTHOR

Quest of the Royal Twins
'Jack Scoltock has a considerable gift for
narrative invention and should be worth
looking for again and again.'
Junior Bookshelf

'Exciting, action-packed adventure.'
Derry Journal

Badger, Beano and the Magic Mushroom
'Wonderfully illustrated . . . a tale oozing magic
and imagination.'
Evening Herald

JEREMY'S ADVENTURE

JEREMY'S ADVENTURE

Jack Scoltock

Illustrated by Aileen Caffrey

WOLFHOUND PRESS

First published 1991 by
WOLFHOUND PRESS,
68 Mountjoy Square,
Dublin 1.

Wolfhound Press receives financial assistance from
The Arts Council (An Chomhairle Ealaíon), Dublin, Ireland.

British Library Cataloguing in Publication Data
Scoltock, Jack
    Jeremy's adventure.
    I. Title
    823.914 [J]

    ISBN 0-86327-305-X

Cover design and illustrations: Aileen Caffrey
Typesetting: Redsetter Ltd., Dublin.
Printed by The Guernsey Press Co. Ltd., Guernsey.

CONTENTS

1

Homecoming

Jeremy's sister gasped with horror, then screamed. The sound of her terrified cry was drowned out as the one-eyed monster came roaring out of the darkness.

The train thundered along the tracks, its bells clanging and steam puffing from its chimney. It roared past them in a flash, almost dragging the two terrified mice along with it.

Cold and frightened, they stared after the train until it disappeared into the snowy darkness. They could still hear its noise as they cautiously made their way across the shiny tracks. Looking to left and right they scampered along the snow-covered, sloping embankment until they found an old rat-path that led up to a concrete bridge. In a few moments they reached the bridge and were on the road. As they scurried along in the snow at the bottom of the high ditches Jeremy looked at his sister. 'We've got to hurry, Marjorie,' he said, 'we must get home tonight.' His nose crinkled worriedly and his sister nodded. They both had the same strange feeling that something was wrong, that their mother was in danger back home.

Many hours later, two tired, hungry mice skirted the town where the bright Christmas lights and decorations twinkled in the moonlight. It was the day before Christmas Eve and it had stopped snowing.

Soon they reached the old rambling shack where their family lived. Before slithering down the disused coal hatch at the side of the shack, Jeremy looked around him. His ears stood up straight as he listened. He frowned, but a few moments later the two mice were inside the coal bunker. Blinking to get their eyes used to the darkness, they headed for a hole no bigger than a golf ball at the back of the bunker. A black spider scurried away as they bent to squeeze inside.

Now they knew for certain that something *was* wrong. Their brothers and sisters were crying, and huddled around a tiny bed in the corner. The bed was a matchbox bed, filled with straw and lying on it was their much-loved father. He was asleep.

'What is it?' asked Jeremy, pushing gently through his brothers and sisters to the bed. 'What's wrong?'

'Father is not well, Jeremy,' sniffed a younger sister.

The brothers and sisters moved closer as Jeremy and Marjorie rubbed at their father's nose with their front paws. He awoke, startled, and, recognising Jeremy and Marjorie, he smiled weakly.

'Father,' whispered Jeremy. 'Are you ill?' Then he looked around the room. 'Where is mother?' he asked.

At this several of his brothers and sisters began to cry again. Jeremy's father sighed and then, moaning softly, he sat upright on the bed. 'It's a long story, son,' he said. There were tears in his eyes now. 'As you know, the weather this winter has been very severe. While you and Marjorie were away helping Aunt Aggy, the snow fell. It was deeper than I can ever remember it. Food was very scarce and your brothers and sisters were always hungry. I went out every day in search of food for them. I was away all of every night and most of every day. I had to search everywhere, you see, even far away. And yet there wasn't enough to feed everyone. I didn't even have enough for myself and so I grew weak and ill. I was so weak that eventually I could not go out to search.' He sighed again. 'Your brothers and sisters could not go out. They are far too young. We would have starved were it not for your mother.' Jeremy's father whispered her name again, tears running down his grey face. Once more the brothers and sisters began to cry.

'Stop!' shouted Jeremy. 'Stop crying and be quiet. I want to hear what has happened, so be quiet.'

'Your mother bravely decided that she had to go out and search for food,' continued his father. 'Ah, Jeremy,' he cried. 'If you only knew how hard I begged her not to go. But it was no use. She knew, and I knew, that she had to go.' Marjorie rubbed at her father's wet nose as tears ran down his face. 'When . . . when she was away I worried all the time until she returned.' With a sniff he reached for the corner of the handkerchief that was his blanket and dabbed at his nose. 'Your mother, as you know, is from a very fine family. She never before had to forage for food. She didn't know about the traps the humans could think up to catch . . . '

'Father!' Jeremy exclaimed. 'You said *didn't*. What do you mean by that?' He glanced at Marjorie, then back to his father. 'Is . . . is mother dead?'

'No, she's not dead . . . not yet . . . ' said his father. Then his voice rose sharply as he cried, 'But she may as well be . . . '

'Father . . . father,' whispered Jeremy, nuzzling into him. 'Please tell us what has happened.'

His father stared at him, then he slid weakly from his bed, saying, 'I'll take you to your mother. But you'll have to be quiet, very quiet.'

Jeremy reached for his father and helped him on to his feet. His father smiled at his younger children. 'You stay here and don't worry. We won't be long.' Turning to his two eldest children he whispered, 'Jeremy, Marjorie, let's go.'

The three moved slowly, and after passing under snow-covered hedges, across moonlit fields, past prowling cats as black as night, they came to the edge of the town. Carol-singing boomed from the town hall as the father led his children down one side of a snow-covered cobbled street. They stopped at an empty house and Jeremy helped his father up the steps and over to a crack at the bottom of a rain spout. It took them three minutes to get up the inside of the spout. They then came to another crack three quarters of the way up and, squeezing through it, they were able to reach the ventilator. A few seconds later all three were inside.

As they came out into the room Jeremy and Marjorie felt the hair on their backs stand straight up. Some sixth sense told them to expect the worst. Then they saw what it was.

Gasping, their tiny eyes took in the horror in front of them. There, lying hardly breathing on a piece of wood, was their poor mother. A square steel spring which was fixed to the wood was squeezing down on her soft, velvety body.

With a loud cry Marjorie hopped towards her.

'Stop! Stop!' Her father's loud shout made her stop at once. Trembling, she turned to him.

'Don't go near her,' whispered her father. 'Stay where you are and don't move.'

'But father,' said Jeremy, staring at his mother. 'Mother is still alive. She's breathing.' Now he moved to go to her.

'Stop!' shouted his father, pulling him back by gripping his son's long tail with his mouth. 'Don't go near her.'

Frowning, Jeremy turned to his father. 'Father,' he whispered, 'Mother is still alive.'

Suddenly, father mouse began to cry. 'I know your mother is still alive, but we can do nothing to help her.

We aren't strong enough to raise the trap. We've tried, all of us. I even had the help of your mother's three strong cousins. You know how strong they are. But even they couldn't budge the trap.' Crying he pawed the air. 'Oh, what can we do? What can we do?' He stared at his poor wife, tears running down his face.

Jeremy looked at Marjorie. She was crying quietly. He looked back again at his mother. How can we free mother? he thought. How? Suddenly it came to him. 'Father,' he whispered. 'What about the Council of Mice? Surely they will know what to do. Let's call a meeting. They will know how to help us.'

Marjorie looked hopefully at her brother. 'Do you think they can, Jeremy?'

'I don't know, Marjorie, but anything is better than doing nothing. Maybe the Council will come up with an idea.' Then, looking at his distraught father, Jeremy said, tearfully, 'Come, father. We are wasting time here. We must return home. We must call a meeting of the Council.'

With a last look at his wife, Jeremy's father allowed himself to be led away from the terrible room.

Back at home, Jeremy and Marjorie gathered their brothers and sisters around them. Their father had been made to lie down again. He watched proudly as Jeremy told the young mice how they could help their mother.

'Now, listen,' he said. 'There is a chance that we can save Mother. But to do that we must get word to the Council of Mice. We will ask them to hold an urgent meeting. You must help us spread the word.'

'Yes, yes,' cried the little mice and they ran off with Jeremy and Marjorie to seek out the Wise Ones.

Within an hour they had returned and Jeremy told his father that a council meeting was to take place in the basement of the old courthouse.

About two thousand mice were already gathered in the basement when Jeremy, his father, and the rest of the family arrived. Standing in the middle of the basement, on top of a pile of law books, were six old white mice. They were the Council of Wise Ones. At the entrance to the basement stood ten of the biggest mice, including Jeremy's mother's three cousins. They were there to guard the basement and watch out for any sign of rats or cats.

The sound of squeaking mice died away as the eldest of the Wise Ones stood on his hind legs and held up one paw.

'We have called an urgent meeting,' he began, 'because one of our tribe is in danger of dying. I will not waste time or upset the Bills family by telling you of their plight. You all know what it is.'

Jeremy and his father nodded grimly as several mice near them looked at them.

'What we want you to do,' said the old mouse, 'is to come up with an idea on how to save poor Mrs Bills. An idea; anything at all. We will listen to what you have to say and if we can think of anything better we will let you know. Now please, I want complete silence, and I must insist that you think out your idea carefully. We do not want to waste time on foolishness. Now think, think hard . . . . '

There was a long silence and Jeremy and his family looked around the basement. Several mice were scratching their heads. Others were staring up at the ceiling as they tried to think. Then to Jeremy's right an old spectacled mouse, with patchy grey skin, stuck up his paw. Everyone listened to what he had to say, but after the Wise Ones had spoken together the idea was turned down.

A few moments later a young mouse raised her paw and gave her idea, but this too was turned down. Then another mouse raised a paw. There were ten ideas altogether but the Wise Ones turned them all down.

Suddenly two paws were raised at the same time. They belonged to twin white mice called Paul and Paula. Together the twins squeaked, 'We think that as there is no one here smart enough to come up with any idea on how to save Mrs Bills, we should ask someone who is wiser than the Wise Ones . . . . '

Eyes widened and loud gasps of hundreds of mice echoed around the basement. Some of the mice grew very angry and squeaked insults at Paul and Paula.

'Well, really!' shouted a cross-looking old mouse. 'What impertinence! Someone wiser than the Wise Ones indeed! There is no one wiser than the Wise Ones . . . . '

Several mice near him nodded in agreement and turned to glare at the twins. The noise grew louder.

'Quiet! Quiet!' shouted the eldest Wise One, stretching higher on his hind legs. All the mice stared at him. 'The twins are right,' he said. The mice gasped with astonishment. Jeremy looked at his father.

'Yes,' shouted the Wise One. 'Paul and Paula are right. We do not have any ideas on how to free Mrs Bills. Therefore we have to seek the advice of someone who is wiser than all of us.'

Paul and Paula nodded, blushing, as they rubbed their crinkled noses together.

'But,' shouted Jeremy. 'If there is no one here wise enough to help us, what can we do?'

Marjorie stared at him, then turned to hear the Wise Ones' reply. The Wise Ones were huddled together, whispering. The squeaking of the other mice grew louder.

A few moments later the eldest of the six Wise Ones scuttled to the edge of the law books again and held up his paw.

'We have come to a decision,' he shouted.

All the mice stared at him.

'Yes. We have decided that there is no one here wise enough to come up with an idea.'

Jeremy let out a sigh and looked at his father. The old mouse looked worriedly back at him.

'But,' shouted the Wise One, 'there is one who could help.'

Now all the mice were quiet.

'Who is it?' shouted Jeremy. 'Tell me'.

'The Wise One looked sadly at Jeremy and said quietly,

'There is one wise mouse who could help you. One who is much older and wiser than any mouse in the land. I am sure that he could help. But he is a long way from here and the journey to him is a dangerous one.'

'Where does he live?' shouted Jeremy.

'Past the Valley of the Owls,' the Wise Mouse said, staring at him.

'The Valley of the Owls!' gasped several mice, their eyes widening with fear.

'And through the Street of Cats,' said the Wise One, his eyes still on Jeremy.

'The Street of Cats,' croaked several mice and nearly all the mice in the basement trembled.

'But first, whoever would seek the wise mouse would have to go through the Rats' Domain . . . . '

'The Rats' . . . Oh no,' whispered an old mouse beside Marjorie.

'And that is the easiest part of the journey,' added the Wise One. Then he paused before saying the next words. 'Whoever would seek the wise mouse would have to go . . . into . . . the Black Building . . . . '

At this all the mice squeaked with fear and several of the young ones fainted.

But Jeremy shouted out, 'Who is this wise mouse who can help us?'

All the Wise Ones looked at Jeremy as the eldest said, 'Galopocus. His name is Galopocus.'

'Galopocus . . . Galopocus . . . Galopocus . . . ' chanted hundreds of mice.

'Whoever would make this journey to seek him out would have to be very brave, and very foolish, even to go near the Black Building,' said the Wise One.

'The Black Building!' whispered the mice. Who would be foolish enough to go near it? they thought.

Suddenly, Jeremy's father pushed through the mice

towards the Wise Ones. 'I will go. It is my problem.' He stopped and looked around him. 'But who will go with me?'

Marjorie and her brothers and sisters watched as Jeremy pushed through to his father, saying, 'Father, you are ill. You cannot make such a long journey. Let me go! You stay with the children!'

His father stared at him, tears filling his eyes. He knew his son was right. He knew he was too ill to go and that someone had to watch over the rest of the family. With tears running down his face he rubbed his nose against Jeremy's, saying, 'Yes, my son, you are right. You must go.' Then looking around the basement at the other mice he shouted, 'Who will go with my son, Jeremy? Who will help him?'

'No, father,' said Jeremy. 'I have to go on my own. It is our problem. Besides, there is no one here who would willingly go near the Black Building.'

Jeremy's father looked around the basement and saw that all the mice were nodding in agreement. He sighed.

Now the Wise Ones stood on the edge of the law books. They raised their paws as the eldest of them said, 'Then the meeting is ended. We all wish young Jeremy a safe journey.'

Looking sadly at Jeremy every mouse in the basement wished him a safe journey. Then they hurried home.

Later, Marjorie said, 'Father, while Jeremy is away, I will be able to go out and find food for all of us. We will be able to feed mother often. We must help to keep her strength up.'

'I am proud of you, my daughter,' her father smiled. 'And of you, son,' he said, turning to Jeremy. 'But you have a long and dangerous journey ahead of you. We will be thinking of you all the time.'

Surrounded by his father and his brothers and sisters, Jeremy rubbed his nose against each of theirs, giving Marjorie a special nuzzle. He was worried and afraid. He knew he must face many dangers. But he did not want to frighten the little ones, so he only smiled and said nothing. When he stood alone with his father he whispered, 'Father, we will save mother. I will be careful and will be back home very soon.'

A few minutes later his father and his brothers and sisters stood at the shack watching sadly as Jeremy slipped through the snow in the direction of the sewers. His little heart was thumping loudly and he was very afraid.

3
The Sewers

Beyond the church at the far end of the town Jeremy slipped through a narrow grating and slid silently, past icicles and snow, into the first sewer. The hairs on top of his ears stood out as he stopped to listen. His heart thumped faster now. He knew that if the rats caught him they would tear him to pieces. He gritted his sharp teeth and splashed silently through the long sewer. He had to get through the Rats' Domain or his mother would die.

Jeremy hurried on through a maze of tunnelled sewers. In the distance he heard the sound of water crashing down. He followed this sound and it became louder and louder until . . . 'A waterfall!' he exclaimed as he came round a corner. The waterfall poured from gratings high above and rushed down into a very big sewer. Jeremy guessed he was going in the right direction now. 'I must get to the end of the big sewer,' he said to himself. 'But how?' A narrow red-bricked path ran along each side of the sewer. Jeremy knew there would be rats on the paths and he would be in trouble. He knew he must go through the deep water of the sewer and not let the rats see him.

Suddenly something caught his sharp eyes. A fine piece of wood bobbing about under the waterfall! The water crashed onto it, lifting it up and down, not letting it slip into the big sewer. Jeremy looked at the wood and thought of a boat. Shivering, he slid into the deep water and swam towards it. He tried to grab the wood, but every time he got near it the water thundered down on top of him and almost flattened him. After a few tries he paddled back from the waterfall and rested. Then he tried again. The water battered him once more, but he reached the bobbing wood and grabbed the edge of it with his teeth. He tried to hold onto it but it was jerked free by the falling water.

After several more attempts Jeremy felt very tired and swam over to the side of the narrow sewer. 'I need a boat,' he cried. 'I need a boat.' As he rested he watched the wood bobbing about. Suddenly the water came crashing down very heavily, so heavily that the wood turned over. Jeremy could see something sticking up from it now. A nail, was it? Yes, a rusty nail! As quick as a flash he was in the water again and going towards the wood. This time he grabbed the nail, held on to it, and dragged the wood back from the waterfall. He pulled his treasure partly out of the water, making sure it would not drift away.

So far, so good! Jeremy then thought of another idea. He returned to a place where he had seen bits of cloth, sticks, paper and other rubbish. He picked out a piece of thin cloth and dragged it back to the wood. Quickly he began to tear it into small pieces. When he thought he had enough pieces he wrapped them around the nail on the wood. Not yet satisfied, he tore more of the cloth into thin strips and hooked these too around the nail. Then he felt ready for his journey through the big sewer. He hoped his plan would work.

Quickly he dragged the wood back into the water and pushed it towards the big sewer. As it picked up speed he scrambled up onto it. Then he pulled the pieces of cloth over him, making sure he was well hidden. Huddled under the cloth, he held on to the nail with his front paws. The wood went faster and faster and soon Jeremy was being carried deep into the sewer.

As he felt himself being whisked along on top of the rushing water, Jeremy peeked out from under his little shelter. He could see hundreds of glowing eyes as the rats scuttled along the slimy paths in search of food. Once Jeremy saw a huge pair of eyes and the black outline of a giant rat. He froze! If it saw him he was finished! He heaved a silent sigh of relief when he saw it turn away and screech at two other rats who were in its way.

Now the wood went faster still and soon Jeremy was being buffeted from all sides. Peeking out again from under his little shelter, he saw far ahead the brightness at the end of the sewer. The wood rushed quickly towards this brightness. Suddenly, with a fierce splash, the pieces of cloth were ripped away, the wood was upended, and Jeremy was thrown into the rushing water. Wow! That was a shock! The end of the sewer looked enormous as he was swept towards it. A few seconds later Jeremy was flying through the air. Looking down, in terror, he saw he was falling into a river. Then, with a splash, he disappeared below.

In the icy water, hardly able to breathe, Jeremy struggled to reach the surface. He found himself floating in the middle of the fast-flowing river. Swimming easily with the water, he waited until he could find a suitable place to swim ashore.

Just ahead he saw a sandy bank and he swam quickly towards it. Soon he was scampering up the bank, trembling with cold. Giving himself a couple of shakes, Jeremy slipped into the long, snow-covered grass. He found himself a cosy place to rest and in a few seconds he was fast asleep.

While he slept Jeremy dreamt about happy times at home. It was springtime once again and the snowdrops and daffodils were in full bloom. He and Marjorie and his little sisters and brothers played in the warm sunlight near

the river. His parents laughed at their games of hide and seek in the long grass. They all picnicked by the side of the river and Jeremy could see how happy and proud and smiling his mother was. Suddenly she was not smiling anymore. She screamed as a monstrous ginger tomcat with many scars on its face came bounding out of the grass. 'Tom! It's Tom! Run! Ruuunnn . . . .' Horrified, Jeremy saw her run into the grass and, ignoring the others, the ginger tomcat took after her.

With a scream Jeremy awoke and knew he had slept too long. He was horrified! He had lost valuable time! He must hurry! Running as fast as he could, he crossed several fields, and at last came to the edge of a great wood. Jeremy began to tremble with fear. In this wood lived the giant owls. In fact, so many owls lived here that it was called the Valley of the Owls. Jeremy knew he would have to get through it before dark. But it was already beginning to get dark! Running harder, he headed into the trees — and into the Valley of the Owls.

4

The Valley of the Owls

Half-way into the wooded valley, Jeremy came to a group of tall oak trees. His eyes narrowed and he stopped. Raising his head, he stretched and sniffed at the air. His sixth sense told him something was wrong. Cautiously he hurried on, sometimes looking up into the trees. He could not see anything to be frightened of. Some light filtered down through the thick branches but it was growing dark.

Jeremy soon came to the deepest part of the valley and, as he moved along a narrow path, he heard it. He stopped immediately, his ears standing straight up. The low howl made the hair bristle all over his body. His eyes widened with fear as he heard the terrible sound again. He remained standing still, his tiny heart thumping. Then he heard the howl once more. The sound seemed to be coming from a hollow of thick weeds just ahead of him. Another loud howl echoed through the trees and this time Jeremy sensed the pain in the sound. Making up his mind, and keeping as low as he could, Jeremy slipped towards the top of the hollow. His nose wrinkled in a pitiful frown when he saw who was letting out the painful howls.

A huge brown and white boxer dog lay there, trapped by his hind legs. The poor dog was chewing at the thick wire that held him. Jeremy could see that he was making his injuries worse by trying to get free.

'He must have been trapped for a long while,' Jeremy

26

said to himself as he saw the boxer roll onto his side and let out another painful howl.

Jeremy knew he should help the dog but his mother had to come first. 'The owls will soon be awake,' he thought. With a quiet sigh he backed away from the hollow and, turning, began to run. He had gone only a few metres when the boxer let out another loud howl. Jeremy stopped. 'I can't,' he exclaimed. 'I can't just leave him there. I have to try to free him.' Retracing his steps he carefully made his way back to the hollow and slid into it.

With a startled growl the boxer rose to his full height and bared his sharp teeth. Then, seeing it was only a tiny mouse, he sank painfully back onto his side, whimpering softly.

'I see you are trapped, boxer,' said Jeremy. 'My mother is trapped too. I don't have much time to help you.'

Jeremy moved towards the boxer's trapped legs but the dog looked scornfully at him and snarled:

'How could a tiny creature like you free me, when I can't free myself?'

Jeremy said nothing but searched through the grass to see where the wire was attached. He soon found that it was fixed to a wooden peg which had been driven deep into the ground near the far end of the hollow. The boxer stared as the little mouse began to nibble at the strong fishing gut and cord which held the wire to the peg.

In a minute Jeremy had bitten through to the wood, and the wire fell away. It was still wrapped around the boxer's legs.

'I'm afraid I can't help you get the wire from your legs,' said Jeremy. 'It's far too strong for me to bite through.'

'And for me too,' said the boxer. 'But at least I can get out of this hollow.'

Jeremy watched as the boxer painfully dragged himself out of the hollow and onto the path. His paws had started

to bleed, but, ignoring the pain, the boxer smiled at Jeremy.

'Thank you, mouse,' he said.

'My name is Jeremy.'

'Thank you, Jeremy. My name is Barry. If you hadn't come along and helped me I might have starved to death.'

Staring at Barry's bleeding legs, Jeremy asked, 'Will you be able to get home like that?'

'Yes,' said Barry. 'I think so. My master will free me. My master is very kind.'

Jeremy smiled up at the big dog, then remembering his mother, he said, 'I have to go. I have to get across the Valley of the Owls before it gets . . . ' He was about to say, 'dark' when, horrified, he realised it *was* dark, very dark. Above him, somewhere in the trees, he heard the terrifying 'hoot, hoot'. The owls were awake.

Barry seemed to understand Jeremy's plight. 'Why don't you come with me?' he said. 'I live on the other side of the Valley of the Owls. I will see you safely through it.'

Jeremy shivered again as he heard the 'hoot, hoot' of a giant owl. Quickly he ran up Barry's front legs and onto his back. The sound of wide wings flapping made him run right up onto Barry's head and into his left ear. He was safe. As Barry set off home, Jeremy told him about his mother.

An hour later they were out of the woods. Peeking out from Barry's ear Jeremy could see the lights of the village and its long, narrow street.

Thanking Jeremy again, Barry added, 'If ever I can be of help to you, just let your Wise Ones know. They will be able to contact me through the Council of Dogs. Well, Jeremy, goodbye! Watch out for those cats! There are lots of cats in the village and even I wouldn't tackle them.'

Jeremy stared after Barry as the boxer hobbled painfully away. Then he turned to look at the village again. It was beginning to snow. He felt very cold, very afraid. He had to go through the village, and in order to do that, he had to go down the Street of Cats. There it was, before him, the dark, snow-covered street of staring eyes and terrible screeches. Trembling, he ran towards it.

5

The Street of Cats

Taking a deep breath and looking to left and right, Jeremy entered the Street of Cats. He kept to the darkest side and slipped quietly along it. He had gone only a few metres when he heard a loud piercing screech behind him. He turned, his heart thumping. Three of the biggest cats he had ever seen were coming down the street.

Jeremy stopped and stared. The big ginger tomcat and the two black cats with him were clearly visible as they walked on the moonlit side of the street. They came closer and Jeremy knew it would be only a few seconds before they saw him. He looked all around for a place to hide. Suddenly out of the corner of his eye he saw some rags lying in a doorway. With his eyes still on the cats, he edged sideways. Then, in a flash, he ran for the rags and dived under them.

'Miaow!' screeched one of the cats. For a heart-stopping second Jeremy thought he was for it! Peeking out he saw the three cats walking past and on down the street.

He lay under the rags, afraid to come out. What can I do? he thought. I have to go down the street. But if I do, those cats are bound to spot me. Oh, what can I do?

Suddenly he felt the rags move and his eyes widened with fear. I've been discovered, he thought, terribly frightened. He lay very still, holding his breath. Nothing

happened. Then the rags moved slightly again and this time Jeremy heard a strange snoring noise.

'Zzzzzzzz . . . '

Jeremy's ears pricked up. He peeked out from under the rags. Beside him lay a bottle. Sniffing, he smelled the foul-smelling liquid.

'Zzzzzzzz . . . '

The snoring noise was followed this time by a snort and the rags moved again. It was then that Jeremy realised that the rags were someone's clothes. A human, a man, and he was sleeping in the doorway! He was drunk!

As he listened to the snores, Jeremy took a look around him. He moved out to the edge of the doorstep and looked up and down the street. Away in the distance he could hear terrible screeching, but there was no sign of cats. Then he stared at the drunk again. The man was lying on his back. His mouth was open. Jeremy was about to leave the doorway when an idea came to him. 'If only,' he said to himself. 'If only the human is going in the direction I want to go!' He trembled as he thought of the three cats. 'I won't stand a chance if they see me. And they're bound to if I go on down the street.' With these thoughts in his head Jeremy looked at the sleeping man again. Slowly he edged towards the man and went right up to his left ear. Then, taking a deep breath, he took a quick nip at the ear and jumped back.

'Zzzzzzzz . . . '

The man's snoring continued as he slept on. Jeremy crept forward again. This time he took a bigger breath, then nipped harder on the man's ear. The man grunted and moaned for a few seconds but very soon his snoring buzzed from the doorway.

'Third time lucky,' said the determined little mouse to himself. Bracing himself, he took the biggest bite yet of the man's ear, then jumped back. With a loud curse the man reached up to his ear and rolled about in the doorway, holding on to it. Jeremy watched and waited and just before the man staggered to his feet the brave little mouse nipped into the pocket of his overcoat. The drunken man, not noticing he had a pocket passenger, stumbled away.

Jeremy looked out from the pocket and smiled. The man was heading down the street!

Jeremy was buffeted about in the pocket. He felt dizzy by the time the man stopped, pushed open a door and went into a house. 'He's home!' said Jeremy to himself.

Throwing his overcoat on the hallstand, the man staggered into the sitting room. Jeremy listened to him talking away to himself for a while, before peeking out of the pocket. A few seconds later he was squeezing under the front door and out into the doorway. Looking up and down the street, he could see he had only two houses to go before he reached the bottom of the Street of Cats. Away back up the street he heard two loud 'miaows' and he heaved a sigh of relief. Then, without hesitating, he leapt from the doorway and raced to the bottom of the street.

Jeremy was very pleased with himself. He suddenly realised how hungry he was, so he searched around for a little food and ate his fill. Then he headed into a field and up towards a hill. When he was half-way up the hill he saw the high wire fence. Beyond it was the dreaded Black Building!

6
Dracula and the Dobermans

Jeremy headed towards a tall chestnut tree which grew about twenty metres from the fence. As he scuttled along he sniffed the air. He could smell dogs.

When he reached the tree he sat at the bottom of its thick gnarled trunk. His heart pounded as he stared at the moonlit Black Building. He was terrified. He had heard, as had every mouse in the land, that something terrible went on in the Black Building. But no animal really knew what it was. All that was really known was that the Black Building gave off a fearful scent.

But I still have to get inside, thought Jeremy, rising and running to the fence. He was just about to slip through one of the small holes in the thick wire netting fence when his ears pricked up. The dog's scent made him back away.

'Grrrrrr . . .' A Doberman tore at him with a loud ferocious growl. Jeremy trembled. He stared through the fence at the guard dog's yellow teeth. The fierce dog snarled, 'If you come in here, mouse, we'll get you. Don't think that you are the first mouse to try to get in here. There were others. Rats too, and a few stupid cats. They didn't last long when my friends and I caught them.' With a sneer the Doberman looked behind him.

Jeremy gasped as he saw three pairs of glowing eyes glaring at him from the bushes on the other side.

'And there are four more of us down near the front

gate,' snarled the Doberman. Suddenly he launched himself at the fence and began to bark. Leaping from the bushes, the other three ferocious guard dogs joined him.

With a frightened squeak Jeremy ran back to the tree and lay there panting with fear.

'Ha, ha, ha, ha, ha . . .'

He shuddered as he heard the four guard dogs laugh. When he looked over the fence again the dogs were nowhere to be seen. But Jeremy knew they were there.

'What am I going to do?' he cried. 'I have to get inside. I have to find Galopocus. I just have to. Even if I am to die in the effort I *must* find Galopocus. I *must* get inside the Black Building. But how? How?'

After a little while Jeremy rose to his feet and went over to the fence again. He peered through into the bushes but he could see no sign of the dogs. Cautiously he stuck his head through the fence and listened. He could hear nothing but he could sense he was being watched. Slowly he pulled his head back out again.

'A wise decision, mouse,' the snarling dog's voice said from the bushes.

Jeremy's eyes widened as he saw the eyes watching him. With a terrified squeak he ran along the edge of the fence. Behind him he could hear the guard dogs laughing again.

A few minutes later Jeremy stood beside another part of the fence. Here the bushes were not so close. Once again he stuck his head inside. He listened. He could not sense the dogs. He listened again, but just as he was about to squeeze inside he heard a shrill cry above him. Startled, he looked up. There on the fence was a tiny creature with one of its thin, black, webbed wings flapping about.

'A bat,' said Jeremy aloud, moving back to get a better look. 'A young bat.'

Sure enough it was a bat and it was stuck fast in one of the gaps in the fence. It gave another shrill cry and flapped its wing wildly.

Jeremy frowned. The bat was hopelessly stuck. Its wing was jammed tight into the small gap. He knew he had to help it. Quickly he climbed up the fence and when he reached the frightened bat he clung to the wire beside it.

'Hallo, can I help you?' he asked.

'Could you, please?' squealed the young black bat. 'I can't get my wing free.'

Jeremy studied the bat's predicament. 'I'd need to bite into your wing a bit to pull it out,' he said. 'It might hurt.'

'It hurts now,' cried the bat. 'Oh, please help me! Do what you have to do to get me free!'

Suddenly a low growl below them made them look down. Horrified, Jeremy saw the four Dobermans. Barking loudly, they sprang up to try to reach the two tiny creatures. The fence bounced back and forth as the fierce dogs jumped against it. Jeremy clung on bravely.

'Please, oh, please help me!' cried the bat. 'My wing is very sore. Please help me!'

Below, the guard dogs barked louder and threw themselves harder at the fence.

Jeremy took a deep breath. Then he stretched his head forward and, gently putting his teeth on the folded part of the bat's wing, he pulled hard. As he did so the four dogs threw themselves at the fence. The massive bounce and Jeremy's pull freed the bat and they both fell to the ground together. Winded, Jeremy stared as the bat fluttered beside him. The guard dogs still threw themselves at the fence, barking loudly.

'Are . . . are you all right, bat?' he asked.

'I . . . I think so,' said the bat, standing up. 'Yes, I think so, indeed.' He smiled and Jeremy saw his mouthful of pointed teeth. 'Thank you very much, er . . . I don't know your name.'

'Jeremy,' said Jeremy, smiling.

'My name is Dracula.'

'Dracula! That's a strange name,' said Jeremy, still smiling.

'Yes, it is, isn't it? I was named after my great, great, great uncle, Dracula. He was a count, you know.'

'Was he?' said Jeremy, staring as the bat let out a shrill shriek.

Then the bat asked, 'Why are you here? It's very dangerous for you to be out at this time of night, you know.'

Jeremy stared at Dracula. He had forgotten that bats eat mice.

As if sensing Jeremy's thoughts, Dracula said, 'Oh, don't worry about me or any bat from now on. You have saved my life. No bat will harm you.'

'How will they know about me?' asked Jeremy.

'We have ways,' said the young bat mysteriously. 'But you never answered my question. Why are you here at this terrible place?'

Jeremy told Dracula why he had to get inside the Black Building.

'But with those guard dogs patrolling inside you will never reach it,' said Dracula. He saw there were tears forming in Jeremy's eyes.

Suddenly Dracula flapped his wings and, without a word, flew away. Jeremy looked up into the dark sky. 'Well, that was nice, I must say,' he exclaimed, a bit angry at Dracula's sudden departure. He looked at the fence again. The dogs were gone. He sighed. 'How am I going

to get near the Black Building, with the dogs guarding it?' he said to himself as he began to walk on around the edge of the fence.

Jeremy had gone only about fifty metres when his sixth sense alerted him to danger. The four loud, shrill shrieks made him tremble.

Suddenly, just in front of him landed four of the biggest black bats he had ever seen. He gasped and stared at them as they flapped their wide, webbed wings. Four pairs of dark eyes glared at him.

7

Inside the Black Building

Jeremy knew it was pointless to run. One of the bats hopped towards him. Her black eyes studied the terrified mouse. Then she said, 'Are you the mouse, Jeremy?'

'Ye . . . yes,' stammered Jeremy.

'You are the mouse who saved my son, Dracula.'

'I . . . yes . . . your son?'

'He has asked me to help you.'

'Help me? How?'

'You wish to get inside the terrible place, don't you?'

'Yes, but . . . '

'Then we can help you. Dracula has told us you wish to find the wise mouse, Galopocus. I can carry you over the fence to the Black Building and we will wait until you come out of it again. That is, if you do come out of it.'

'Yes,' said Jeremy thoughtfully, wondering how the bat was going to carry him.

'I will carry you by the tail if that is all right with you,' said Dracula's mother, before Jeremy could ask. 'My sisters here will fly with me in case I let you fall. Is that all right with you?' she repeated.

Jeremy looked back at his long tail. He flicked it left and right and curled it right up. He nodded.

Without another word, Dracula's mother reached for Jeremy's tail with her sharp teeth. Then, flapping her webbed wings, she rose into the air. Her three sisters looked up as she flew over the fence, carrying Jeremy by his tail. Then they flew after her. Far below Jeremy saw one of the guard dogs staring up at them. It barked angrily. Jeremy's heart thumped with fear. He was moving so fast through the air — and so high up!

Now Dracula's mother hovered above the Black Building. 'Where would you like me to leave you?' she asked.

Looking down, Jeremy saw three tall chimneys.

'Leave me on the roof,' he said, gritting his teeth. His tail was beginning to ache. 'I'll manage from there.'

A few moments later, her wings flapping harder, the huge bat dropped Jeremy lightly onto the bottom of the snow-covered, slated roof near the spouting.

'Thank you,' shouted Jeremy as the four bats flew up into the sky.

'We will wait on yonder chestnut tree to see if you come out again. But you will have to hurry. It is not long to dawn. We won't be here when dawn breaks,' shrieked Dracula's mother.

Jeremy watched the four bats fly towards the chestnut tree and disappear into the branches. Seconds later they were hanging upside-down, waiting for Jeremy to return from the Black Building.

At the bottom of the slippery roof, Jeremy looked up at the tall, yellow chimney pots. That would be the quickest way inside, he thought. Then slithering up the roof at an angle, he quickly reached the chimneys. He scrambled up the rough bricks of the middle pot and soon he was standing on the edge of it. The wind was getting stronger and it had started to snow again. He looked down. Below in the darkness he could see nothing. He shivered as another gust of wind threatened to blow him off the pot. Then, remembering his mother, he looked down into the sooty blackness.

A sickening feeling of something terrible seemed to belch up from inside the Black Building, but bravely Jeremy crept into the inside of the chimney pot. Clinging to the soft, sooty sides of the chimney, he moved to the first bend. Soot clogged his nose and eyes and he sneezed several times before he reached it.

By the time he came to the second bend Jeremy could hear terrible crying. His heart pounded and he stopped. The horror of the cries made him widen his eyes and more soot went into them. He sneezed again as more soot puffed up his nose.

He went on downwards and soon came to the inside of the fireplace. The terrible cries were louder now and he stopped to rest on a tiny ledge. The hair all over his body was standing straight out as the dreadful cries grew louder.

More soot fell onto the tiled hearth as the little mouse dropped out of the chimney. Covered in soot, he took a look around him. He was in an office, a cosy office with a table, a chair and an electric fire. But Jeremy had no time to rest. Again, the terrible cries came to him and, giving himself a good shake, he ran to the door. Several sooty pawprints dotted the carpet behind him. In a moment he had squeezed under the door.

Looking up and down the dark corridor, Jeremy listened carefully. The cries were even louder here. He began to move slowly down the corridor and as he passed the first door his sixth sense told him that there were animals inside. Taking a deep breath, he slipped under the door and in the semi-darkness he stared around him. A small, red light glowed from the ceiling and, as his eyes grew accustomed to the light, he gasped at the horror in the room.

8
The Rooms

Cages of rabbits lay on low tables all along each side of the huge room. Many of the rabbits were crying. Horrified, Jeremy could see why. Some of those near him had only one eye. Several white rabbits had a paw missing. Most of them were without their tails and some were completely blind. There were cages and cages of rabbits, and all of them were in great pain.

Gasping with pity, the tearful little mouse scooted up onto the nearest table and looked at the cage there. It was packed with young black-and-white rabbits. They all began to cry when they saw Jeremy.

'Oh . . . oh, help us, little mouse!' cried a tiny hare, much louder than the others. 'Please help us to get out of here! Please . . . please . . . .'

With tears running down his face Jeremy studied the catch on the cage. It would take several mice to open it, he thought.

'I . . . I can't,' he sniffed.

Then a sturdy female rabbit hopped to the front of the cage. 'You have to help us!' she cried. 'You can't leave us in here! Please . . . '

Jeremy stared at the rabbit's good eye. 'What happened to all of you?' he asked. 'Who did these terrible things to you?' He gasped as he saw a rabbit roll over and curl up, crying with pain.

'They . . . they did,' cried an older rabbit.

'They? You mean the humans? But why?' asked Jeremy, in horror.

'They are using us to test their make-up and shampoo,' said the biggest rabbit in the cage. His left ear was missing.

'Make-up? Shampoo? What is that?' asked Jeremy.

'It's the stuff the humans put on their faces and use to wash their hair,' cried one of them. 'It's supposed to make them beautiful.'

'But why are they testing this . . . this make-up and shampoo on you?' asked Jeremy. 'Why don't they test it on themselves?'

'Because, mouse,' snapped an old rabbit, pushing three young hares out of the way to get to the front of the cage, 'some of the stuff is harmful to humans. That is why they test it on us. You can see how . . . Ooowww . . . '

Suddenly the rabbit fell to the floor of the cage and the others watched as he cried out with pain.

'But look what it's doing to you,' whispered a horrified Jeremy. 'Can't the humans see it's killing you?'

'Yes,' cried one of the female rabbits. 'But they don't care. They don't care how we suffer, just as long as they are beautiful. Oh, mouse,' she cried, 'there must be some way you can help us. There has to be. We would be better off dead than . . . . '

Tears ran down Jeremy's face. How can I help them? he thought. How? Then once more he remembered he had to find Galopocus.

'Do any of you rabbits know where Galopocus, the wise mouse, is? I have to find him.'

The rabbits looked at each other.

'Galopocus, the wise mouse?' said the old rabbit. 'No, we have not seen him. I have heard of him though. He is the wisest mouse in all the land, but I thought he was dead.'

'Dead!' said Jeremy. 'No, he can't be. I have come to seek his help. I have to save my mother. He can't be dead. He's supposed to be here . . . somewhere . . . . ' Jeremy looked around the room. All he could see were cages of rabbits.

'You could try the next room,' said the old rabbit, nodding to a door at the bottom of the room. 'They keep the rats in there. Galopocus could be with them.'

'The next room?' said Jeremy. 'How many rooms are there?'

'We don't know,' snapped the old rabbit. 'But there are dogs, cats, mice, rats and rabbits here. There could be others. There are many rooms . . . many rooms . . . . ' He moaned with pain as he sniffed at the air.

'I . . . I need to find Galopocus,' whispered Jeremy, backing away. 'I have to go.' In a second he was on the floor. Sniffing to hold back his tears, he ran to the door at the bottom of the room.

'Help us . . . Please help us!' The cries of the rabbits followed him as he squeezed under the door and into the next room.

Harsh painful squeals and scuffling told Jeremy he was now in a room full of rats. He shuddered. The room was the same size as the rabbits' room, with even more cages. Rats of every colour and size paced up and down their cages. Many of them were squealing with pain. Several lay on their sides, their paws prodding the air. Others lay motionless. The squeals grew louder as Jeremy ran to the middle of the room and scooted up onto one of the tables. Several hunched rats glared at him as he came closer to their cage. The huge rats sniffed and one of them tore at the cage door with his sharp teeth and claws, trying to get at Jeremy. The frightened mouse moved quickly back from the cage.

'What are you doing in here?' snapped an old black rat, crawling to the front of the cage.

'I'm looking for Galopocus, the wise mouse,' said Jeremy. 'Do you know where he is?'

'That old fool!' snapped another rat, licking at its injured paws.

Jeremy gasped with horror as he saw that some of the rats had lost their tails. At the back of the cage he could see two tails lying in the corner.

'What do you want him for?' snapped the rat who had spoken first.

'To . . . to help me save my mother,' said Jeremy, still looking at the tails.

'He'll help no one where he is,' sneered the youngest and biggest of the rats.

'Where is he?' asked Jeremy, moving closer to the cage.

'How should I know?' snapped the rat. 'And anyway, why should I tell you. You're only a mouse and . . . ohhhh . . . . '

Suddenly the young rat fell onto his side and curled into a ball, crying out in pain.

Jeremy gasped with pity. 'Did . . . did they test you too?' he asked.

'Yes,' sighed the oldest of the rats who had not moved but lay on his side near the two tails. 'All of us.'

Jeremy moved away from the cage and took a look around the room. It was a terrible sight. Every rat was staring at him. Then away at the back of the room a young black rat cried out, 'Won't you help us escape, mouse? Please . . . '

'Please . . . please . . . ' several other young rats cried.

The rats' cries grew louder. With a sigh Jeremy jumped onto the floor and scooted down the room to the door. As he stood there getting ready to squeeze under the door, he heard the rats' pitiful cries.

'Please . . . please, help us! Help us! Please . . . '

With tears in his eyes, he bent and squeezed into the next room.

As soon as he came into the room Jeremy felt his skin crawl. He smelled the dreaded scent of cats, many cats. There must have been more than five hundred of them in the room. But Jeremy was safe because all the cats were in cages. Some of the cages lined the centre of the floor and, as Jeremy passed, several huge, striped cats shot their paws through the cage, trying to grab him.

He stopped in front of a cage which held two monstrous ginger tomcats. They spat at him. But then one of them scraped his front paw slowly along the floor of the cage. He miaowed painfully and his tail curled back and forth. Spitting at Jeremy again, the other tomcat screeched, 'What are you doing out of your cage?'

'My cage? But I wasn't in a cage,' said Jeremy.

'Then what do you want? Miaow!'

Suddenly the big cat screamed and rolled over on its side. 'Miaow!' It rolled about in agony for a few seconds. Then it slowly staggered back onto its feet.

'What do you want in here with us cats?' he asked, his yellow eyes glaring at Jeremy.

'I'm looking for Galopocus.'

'Him,' sneered the tomcat, scraping the floor with his claws. 'The wise mouse, hah! He'll not be wise for much longer if I get my claws on him.'

Jeremy stared at the two tomcats. All around him he could hear the other cats crying. Then he saw the tomcat roll over again and miaow painfully.

'Did the humans do tests on you too?' Jeremy whispered sadly.

'What do you think?' snarled the other tomcat, looking at his companion. 'Of course they did. They still do. Every day they come in here and stick needles in us. They smear stuff on our faces and eyes. Shampoo, I think it is called. But the long, sharp needles are the worst; needles with hateful liquid in them.' The tomcat shuddered. 'The pain is terrible. Do you know that over one hundred of us have died this year?'

'One hundred!' gasped Jeremy.

'Yes, and there will be five more on Christmas Eve. Well, maybe not. The humans have gone home for Christmas. Home to eat their fill, while we stay here to starve and suffer.'

Jeremy trembled as he saw the tomcat lick his lips and stare hungrily at him. Backing away, the little mouse stammered, 'I . . . I have to be going now.' Soon he was dodging past the reaching claws, and on to the bottom of the room.

'Can't you please stay and free us?' Jeremy heard a tiny black-and-white kitten cry. 'Please . . . . '

'No, I . . . I have to help my mother,' shouted Jeremy. 'I have to find Galopocus.'

He squeezed into the next room.

This room was the biggest so far and Jeremy was shocked to find hundreds of pups lying in three huge cages. There were all kinds of pups in there — labradors, Great Danes, red setters, cocker spaniels, St Bernards, pointers, Irish wolfhounds. Several of them jumped to their feet when they saw Jeremy, their tails wagging vigorously. Others just lay there, so weak they could not even open their eyes. Some very young pups were crying and four St Bernards lay licking their sore paws.

'Hallo,' whispered Jeremy, looking sadly at the pups

crowded at the front of the middle cage. 'Could you tell me where I can find Galopocus, the wise mouse?' He stared, horrified, at two white terriers who were licking at big red sores in their sides.

'Gal . . . Gal . . . ' one of them stammered.

'Galopocus, the wise mouse. Could you please tell me where I can find him?'

'A mouse, you say?' whined a red setter.

'Yes,' said Jeremy. 'The wisest mouse in the land.' He looked at a dachshund who had running sores in both his eyes. 'Do you know where he is?'

'There are mice in the next room. I saw them when the humans opened the door to come in and put the horrible stuff on our eyes,' the dachshund said.

'The next room,' said Jeremy. 'Thank you!'

He was running off to the bottom of the room when he heard a setter say, 'Mouse, when you leave here, could you take a message to my father?'

'Your father?' said Jeremy. 'But I don't know where he lives. What's his name?'

'Arthur. If you see him could you tell him . . . tell him,' the little setter cried, broken-hearted, 'that mother died. They killed mother. Tell him that Tommy told you.'

Jeremy sniffed as he saw the tears running down Tommy's face. He went over to the pup's cage, stuck his nose through and rubbed it against the setter's nose. As he did so a black labrador pup cried, 'Please try to get us out of here . . . . '

'Oh, but I can't,' said Jeremy, backing away. 'How can I? I have to get on. I have to find Galopocus. My mother needs help. I have to get on . . . . '

As he ran down the floor he felt the tears sting his eyes, and as he slipped under the door he heard the gentle voices of the pups crying, 'Goodbye'.

9
Galopocus

The familiar smell of mice reached Jeremy when he came into the room. Fifty cages lay on tables on each side of the room and each cage was packed with mice.

Quickly, Jeremy scrambled up onto the table that held a cage of grey mice. There in front of him was a pitiful sight. About fifteen young mice lay at one side of the cage, on their sides. The smell reached Jeremy as he stared at them. Horrified, he knew some of them were dead.

Now the other mice saw him as he ran up to the cage door. In a moment they were pushing against the wire door crying, 'Please help us! Let us out . . . . '

Jeremy looked at the nearest mice. Some of them had only one ear. Others had no tails. Nearly all of them had sores on their faces and some had only one eye.

Sniffing, as the tears ran down his face, Jeremy whispered, 'Do you know where I can find Galopocus?'

Immediately the mice grew silent and, turning, they stared to the bottom of the room.

'He's down there,' squeaked a mouse with one ear. 'He's very ill.'

Jeremy hopped from the table and ran to the bottom of the room. A large cage lay on a table near the door. In it was the biggest mouse Jeremy had ever seen. It was Galopocus. He was completely white. His eyes were closed and he lay on his side, hardly breathing. Jeremy saw the needle holes all over his patchy skin.

'Galopocus! Galopocus!' whispered Jeremy. 'Wake up! Please wake up!'

The old mouse opened his eyes, and when he saw Jeremy standing outside his cage he struggled painfully to his feet.

'I wasn't sleeping, young one,' he croaked. 'I never sleep now.' He frowned. 'How did you get out of your cage?'

'I didn't,' said Jeremy, coming closer to the cage. 'I came from outside. I need your help. You see, my mother . . . .'

'Easy, easy, young one. Start from the very beginning. Tell me who you are. Tell me everything.'

'My name is Jeremy,' said the little mouse and he told Galopocus all that had happened to his mother and how he came to the Black Building.

Galopocus's old eyes studied him. 'You're a very brave mouse, young one,' he said quietly.

Suddenly he gasped and his legs collapsed under him. Horrified, Jeremy saw him fall over onto his side, moaning painfully.

'Ughhhh, the pain is getting worse,' the old mouse gasped as he struggled to his feet again. Frowning at Jeremy, he listened to the cries of the other mice. 'Jeremy,' he whispered, 'Come closer.'

Jeremy pressed his nose right up against the door of the cage, and listened to the old, wise mouse.

'Jeremy,' Galopocus whispered. 'You have to get help to free all the animals in this dreadful place.'

'Me!' exclaimed Jeremy, aghast. 'But how? How can I do that? Besides, I must hurry home to save my mother. You haven't told me how I can save her.'

Galopocus sighed, then said, 'The answer to your problem lies in your journey here. You saved a boxer.

He owes you his life. He is bound by the dogs' code to help you. He will be strong enough to raise the steel trap. He will help you save your mother.'

Jeremy smiled as he thought about this. 'Yes,' he said. 'Barry will help me. Why didn't I think of that? Thank you, Galopocus.'

'Jeremy,' whispered Galopocus, pressing his face against the door, 'it is your duty to try to save your brethren. You have to get help after you free your mother.'

'Help? But . . . ?'

'Every animal in the Black Building must be freed.'

'Every animal?' gasped Jeremy. 'Surely you don't mean the cats? And the rats?'

'Every animal,' repeated Galopocus firmly.

'But . . . but . . . the cats,' stammered Jeremy. 'They are our enemies.'

'No, not in here. They are suffering just like the mice. They have to be freed with the rest of the animals.'

'But how? I . . . I'm only a small mouse . . . .'

Galopocus groaned again with pain but stayed on his feet. 'Jeremy,' he gasped. 'You must get all the animals to hold a great meeting. You must tell them the terrible things that are going on in here. Tell them what you have seen. Tell them we will all die if they don't help to free us. Tell them that the humans are away for Christmas. Jeremy, there has to be a Council of Animals.'

Jeremy's eyes widened. 'A Council of Animals? Of all the animals, you mean? But Galopocus, the cats would kill us if we attended such a council.'

No,' whispered Galopocus. 'Not if an Animal Truce is called.'

'Truce? What is that?' asked Jeremy.

'An Animal Truce was called many years ago,' explained the old mouse. 'It lasted a long time. If an

Animal Truce is called it means that every animal in the land is bound to obey it. No animal can harm another until the Animal Truce is over. Jeremy, tell them that the humans are testing things on us. Tell them we will all be dead soon. Tell them the Black Building has to be destroyed. I will show you how to do that.'

Jeremy stared at Galopocus. Then, remembering the short time he had to save his mother, he said, 'Galopocus, I will try to do what you want. I will tell my council what you have told me. I will tell them what I have seen. Maybe they can contact the other animals. Barry told me that if I needed his help, our council was to contact his. The dogs might be able to get the cats and rats to join them. I don't know, but I'll try. I will certainly try. But I have to go now. I have to save my mother.'

Galopocus watched as Jeremy ran to the edge of the table. Before hopping down from it Jeremy turned and looked back at the wise old mouse. 'Goodbye, Galopocus! Thank you!' he said. But just then Galopocus fell over onto his side and moaned with pain. Gritting his teeth, Jeremy turned away, leapt to the floor and ran as fast as he could up to the top of the room. In a minute he had raced through all the rooms and was back in the office.

Breathing hard Jeremy reached the top of the chimney. Before calling for the bats he stood there. His body ached all over and his tail was sore. The horror of what he had seen inside the terrible building numbed his brain. He was exhausted. But remembering the urgency of getting help to his mother, he called. He gritted his teeth to keep from crying with pain as Dracula's mother carried him by his tail from the roof, out over the fence, over the village, past the valley of the owls and on to the outskirts of the town. Just when he thought he could stand the pain no longer Dracula's mother landed, releasing Jeremy at once. Jeremy slid for a few seconds before he could get to his feet. He looked for Dracula's mother to thank her but she was already flying back to her family. Blinking his tired eyes he headed towards the shack. It was beginning to snow when he slid down into the coal bunker.

As he staggered inside he was immediately surrounded by his happy family. His father studied him before speaking. He's exhausted, he thought. Then he asked, 'Did you see him? Did you see Galopocus?'

'Yes, father,' Jeremy said, 'and he told me to get help from Barry boxer. You see, I was able to save Barry boxer from a rabbit trap. Barry promised help if ever I needed it.' Jeremy yawned and rubbed his eyes. He was very tired, so his father gently pushed him onto his bed and began to pat straw around him. 'Father,' whispered Jeremy, 'we must save *them* too.'

'Who, Jeremy? Who?' Jeremy's father asked. His son was asleep. 'What must he have been through?' he said to himself. Then he turned to Marjorie and asked her to take a message to the Wise Ones. 'Tell them what you have heard. Tell them about this Barry boxer. Tell them he is bound to help Jeremy.'

Marjorie ran off and, a few minutes later, met up with one of the Wise Ones. He listened to her story and then he said, 'We must get word to the Council of Dogs and tell them of this. We must tell them that Jeremy needs the boxer's help.'

Two hours after the sun had risen, four mice and a dog found their way into the room where Jeremy's mother lay trapped. They were Mr Bills, Jeremy, Marjorie, one of the Wise Ones, and Barry Boxer. Jeremy looked at Marjorie and his father. 'Mother is still breathing,' he said, hopefully.

'Now,' whispered the Wise One. 'This is what you must do . . . . '

He quickly told Barry his plan. Barry limped towards the trap. He carefully placed one of his front paws on the wooden part of the trap. Then, bending his huge head, he bared his strong teeth and gripped the steel spring. With a low growl, he pulled.

Suddenly the trap slipped and hit one of his bandaged paws. With a yelp, Barry let go of the spring.

'Easy, dog,' shouted the Wise One. 'Try again. This time put both your front paws on the trap. One on the back of it and one on the side.'

Barry raised his eyes and looked at Jeremy as if to say, sorry. But he did as the Wise One told him. When he was in position he bent once more and grabbed the spring. Then he carefully raised his head and, yes, the spring lifted!

Quickly, as Barry held the spring, Jeremy helped pull his mother free. Then Barry gently eased the spring back into place and stepped away from the trap. Mrs Bills lay on the floor. Her husband wet his paws and placed one of them on her mouth. With the other he gently dabbed at her eyes. With a soft groan she opened her eyes and looked up. She gave a start when she saw the huge dog towering over her. But when she saw her husband and her son and daughter, smiling, with tears in their eyes, she relaxed and smiled too.

'I think she'll be fine now, friends,' said Barry. 'So I'll be off. I'll bring some food over to you later on.' He smiled at Jeremy. 'Then I will have paid my debt to you, my friend.'

Jeremy smiled back at him and they watched as his mother rose to her feet and set out for home, with the help of her husband and daughter.

As the Wise One and Barry prepared to go, Jeremy

said, 'Barry, I have need of your help again. There is something I must tell you, and you, Wise One.' He turned to the old mouse.

The big boxer frowned, the skin over his bright eyes wrinkling over them. 'What is it, Jeremy?' He studied Jeremy's serious face.

'Come on. I'll tell you on the way home.'

10

Decisions

Near a hollow by the snow-covered railway track Jeremy told Barry and the Wise One about life in the Black Building. He cried as he described what he had seen and heard there. When he had finished his story the Wise One said, 'And Galopocus asked you to get all the animals to hold a great council?'

'Yes,' said Jeremy. 'And he told me they will have to hurry because there is not much time. He said the humans are on holiday for Christmas. They will be back soon.'

The Wise mouse thought about what Jeremy had told him. He shivered. 'There will have to be a Council of Animals,' he said. 'But first we must hold a very urgent meeting of the Council of Mice. Yes, a meeting of the Council of Mice must come first.'

Jeremy, his parents and his brothers and sisters stood near the front of the packed basement. More than five thousand mice, along with Barry boxer, were gathered there. The noise of the squeaking mice made Barry bark loudly. Then one of the six Wise Ones held up his paw. The mice immediately became quiet. They knew there had to be a very important reason for this urgent meeting. And besides, a dog had never before been invited to the council.

'This is the most urgent meeting of all our meetings,'

said the Wise One who had heard Jeremy's story. 'The wisest mouse in all the land needs our help. He has asked us to call this very urgent meeting of our council.'

'Galopocus! Galopocus!' The whispered name echoed around the basement.

'Yes,' shouted the Wise One. 'Galopocus, and he is suffering. Suffering along with hundreds of other mice and other animals. Suffering like the cats, the rats, the rabbits, and the dogs. All suffering terrible pain in that dreadful place, the Black Building.'

He waited until this information had sunk in. Then he shouted, 'We have to free him. We have to free *all* the animals in the Black Building.'

'*All* the animals?' squeaked an old grey mouse from the back of the basement. 'Surely you don't mean the *cats*?'

'No, no, not the cats,' shouted a tiny white mouse, looking very faint.

'Yes,' shouted the Wise One. 'I do mean the cats, and the rats . . . . '

'Nooooooo,' squeaked several hundred mice.

'All of them must be saved,' squeaked the Wise One. 'And the Black Building must be destroyed. That is what Galopocus has asked of us. We cannot let him down.'

'But . . . but how are we going to do this?' cried a young mouse standing beside Barry's left front paw. 'We are only mice.'

'We will not be doing it on our own. Galopocus wants all the animals to hold a meeting together. He wants a Council of Animals to be held.'

When he said this the mice became very quiet.

'Yes,' the Wise One continued. 'With the help of Barry boxer here we Wise Ones will first meet the Council of Dogs and then we will see what we can do to meet the other animals.'

'But . . . but the cats?' cried a fearful mouse. 'They will kill us . . . . '

'And the rats. Don't forget about them,' squeaked another.

'They will not harm us,' said the Wise One, 'if Jeremy can tell them what terrible things their own are suffering in the Black Building.' Then he spoke to the boxer. 'Barry, would you be kind enough to take Jeremy along to your council now? He must tell them about what is going on in the Black Building. Maybe when they hear about those terrible things they will arrange meetings with the cats and the others.'

Jeremy smiled at the big dog, hopped onto his back, and then they were on their way.

It was a crispy, bright day and the countryside was covered with snow. Barry and Jeremy headed along the railway track until they came to a long, dark tunnel.

At the entrance to the tunnel Barry raised his head and let out a long, low howl. The eerie sound echoed into the tunnel. Jeremy was scared. He hopped off Barry's back and stood beside him. A loud growl came back from the tunnel and a few seconds later the little mouse was staring at two of the dirtiest dogs he had ever seen. The bigger dog was a brown-and-white terrier. One of its ears was chewed and it had two long scars on its brown face. The other dog was a poodle. It should have been white but it was so dirty it looked brown. It was covered in thick, curly hair.

'Hello, Barry,' growled the terrier. 'What brings you here at this time of day?' He glared at Jeremy who crouched by Barry's right front paw. 'What's up with the rodent?'

Barry smiled at Jeremy. 'He's my friend, Towser. He saved my life. But that is not why we are here. I have come to ask you to call an urgent meeting of the council.'

'An urgent meeting? You'll have to have a very good reason to make me do that,' growled Towser.

'I have,' said Barry. Then turning to Jeremy, he said, 'Jeremy, perhaps you should tell Towser and Fifi what you have seen in the Black Building.'

'The Black Building!' whispered Fifi, with fear in her voice.

'Yes, we have heard of the Black Building,' said Towser, looking very serious. 'Tell us the whole story.'

The call went out to every dog in the land, and within an hour more than one thousand dogs were crowded into the huge, disused, train tunnel.

Above, hiding in a hole in the red-bricked roof, two black rats watched with beady eyes and listened to everything.

Jeremy stood with five dogs on a low, red-brick platform at the closed end of the tunnel. He felt very nervous. Beside him were two Irish wolfhounds and a Great Dane. Towser and another dog stood behind him.

Dogs of every breed and size had gathered in the tunnel. They stood with their tongues hanging out, wondering why this urgent meeting had been called. Their barking and howling stopped as one of the wolfhounds raised a huge paw.

'Be quiet!' he growled. 'Be quiet! What I have to tell you is of great importance. This meeting was called at the request of the Council of Mice, through Barry boxer and because of Jeremy mouse.' He turned to Jeremy who looked nervously at the angry dogs.

'A mouse!' roared an Afghan hound. 'You're telling me that this meeting has been called because of a rodent?'

'Oh, be quiet, Dan!' roared the Great Dane, 'and listen! When Jeremy has finished you can do your complaining if you want to.'

Dan scowled and his long, skinny tail whipped up and down irritably.

'You'd better begin, Jeremy,' said Towser.

When Jeremy had finished his story there were tears in his eyes. Several dogs looked shocked.

Suddenly Dan growled, 'How do we know he is telling the truth?'

Jeremy grew angry at this. 'I don't tell lies,' he squeaked. 'I *am* telling the truth. What would I have to gain by lying to you?'

The Great Dane, whose name was Shane, glared at Dan and then barked, 'Well, canine friends, what do you think we should do? This wise mouse Galopocus has asked for a Council of Animals. A council of dogs, cats, rabbits, rats, and mice — all the animals who have friends in the Black Building. We would have to agree not to harm each other until we have freed each of our own from that hateful place.'

Suddenly a short-legged, burly bulldog let out a loud growl. 'It will be hard not to attack the cats.'

'Yes, it will, Odin,' barked one of the wolfhounds. 'But you will have to keep from attacking all animals. Look, friends,' he shouted, 'we could be the next animals to be tested in the Black Building. Or even worse, one of our young could be taken and tested. I'd rather die than let any of my family suffer in that place. No, it is time we took a stand against the humans.'

Suddenly Jeremy remembered the young setter called Tommy. With a small cough he interrupted the wolfhound. 'Could I ask the red setters if any of them is called Arthur?'

One of a group of setters near the back of the tunnel

shouted, 'I'm called Arthur.'

'You have a son called Tommy . . . . '

'Tommy,' cried the setter. 'You saw Tommy?'

'Yes,' squeaked Jeremy sadly. 'He told me . . . he told me to tell you that his . . . his mother had died . . . . '

'Nooooooo . . . ' howled Arthur. 'Nooooo . . . ' The other setters gathered around him, licking the tears from his face.

'I think that proves Jeremy was telling the truth,' hissed Shane, glaring at Dan who hung his head, ashamed. Then, looking out over the other dogs, Shane barked, 'There has to be a Council of Animals.'

'Yesssssss . . . Yesssssss . . . ' roared all the dogs.

Above, the two rats, who had seen and heard everything, slipped through holes in the bricks and on to the road. Soon the biggest sewer in the town was packed with rats. The two rats called a meeting of the Council of Rats because of what they had seen and heard in the tunnel.

Later, word was sent to the Irish wolfhounds that the rats would attend a Council of Animals.

A ginger tomcat and two white Persian cats were walking up the Street of Cats when they heard a low growl. The hair stood up on their backs but, unafraid, they moved closer together. They glared with slanted, wicked eyes when they saw Towser and Fifi.

'Tom,' growled Towser. 'Could I speak to you for a few minutes, please?'

The big tomcat eyed Towser. He grinned as he recognised the terrier. One of the scars on Towser's face had been caused by himself. 'Speak with me? That's a new one. What do you want?' he spat.

'It's very important,' said Towser.

'Important?' screeched one of the Persians. 'How important?'

'It will take just a few minutes to explain why I am here,' said Towser.

The three cats looked at each other. Then they studied Towser and Fifi. They looked at each other again and nodded.

'Ok, Towser, explain,' said Tom. 'But stay just where you are.'

Sitting down, Towser began.

'And you say there are hundreds of our feline friends suffering in the Black Building?' asked Tom, studying Towser carefully.

'Yes, and rats and dogs, and rabbits and mice . . . . '

'Mice!' spat Tom, glaring at Towser, tearing through the hard snow with his claws. 'We do not care about mice. It is our own kind we want to rescue. Mice are for eating, not rescuing.'

'They are all to be rescued,' snapped Towser. 'Every animal in the Black Building is suffering. *All* of them must be rescued and the hateful place must be destroyed.' Giving Tom one of his most piercing looks, he growled, 'If not, you could end up there yourself.'

The big cat narrowed his eyes. He shivered. He could not imagine being locked up and having the humans put horrible stuff on his face and eyes. He shivered again, then said, 'I will call a meeting of the Council of Cats. It will be up to them to decide what we will do.'

'Fair enough,' said Towser, standing up. 'But make sure the meeting is held soon. We hope to have a Council of Animals tonight.'

Barry stood at the entrance to the biggest rabbit hole on the edge of the town and shouted down into it. 'Rabbits, we know you are down there. This is Barry boxer speaking. With me is Jeremy mouse. He saved my life.' Barry smiled at Jeremy who smiled back at him. 'You do not have to be afraid, rabbits,' Barry shouted down the rabbit hole again. 'Please listen to what Jeremy mouse has to tell you. And please believe him.'

Jeremy moved just inside the hole and shouted down everything he had seen in the Black Building. When he was finished Barry said, 'Rabbits, I would ask you to call a meeting of the Council of Rabbits. When your council has talked about all we have told you, tell them that there is to be a meeting of the Council of Animals at midnight.'

As they walked home Jeremy asked Barry, 'Do you think the rabbits will hold a meeting of their council?'

'They'll have to,' growled Barry. 'If they have any love for their own kind they'll have to.' Then, smiling at Jeremy, he said, 'Well, Jeremy, I'll leave you off at the shack. I'll see you at the Council of Animals tonight.'

As mouse and dog headed towards the shack they sensed the air buzzing with the silent call of the animals. Rabbits scattered all over the countryside stood still, their ears pricked up as their sixth sense told them there was to be a meeting. Rats, deep in the sewers, stopped what they were doing as they too heard the call. Soon all the animals knew about the meeting of the Council of Animals, and where and when they should turn up.

In a warren the size of the inside of a small chapel, thousands of rabbits and hares had a meeting.

'But who will protect us from the dogs and the cats?'

snuffled a tiny white rabbit.

'The dogs have promised we won't be harmed,' said Iggy, the biggest hare in the warren.

'Dogs, hah!' snuffled an old rabbit with patchy, brown fur. 'You can't trust them.'

'I think we can this time,' said Iggy, his pink eyes looking around the warren.

Iggy thought about what Jeremy had told them. He could hardly believe the story of the Black Building and the suffering the animals were going through. But he remembered that a large number of rabbits had gone missing of late. His own young niece and his wife's cousin had disappeared during the warm days. He had suspected the humans had taken them.

'Listen to me,' he shouted after a while. 'You have heard how much our own kind are suffering. We have to help the other animals to rescue them and destroy the Black Building. If you agree, I will send word that we will go to the Council of Animals after dark. But the cats, the dogs, the rats, and the mice must take the Animal Truce.'

'Animal Truce? What is that?' snuffled a young hare.

'I remember,' said an old brown rabbit, 'many years ago when the dreaded disease struck down thousands of our kind. We asked the Council of Animals for an Animal Truce then. It lasted a year.'

'And what happened?' asked the young hare.

'The dogs, the cats and the rats left us alone for a full year. Not one rabbit or hare was killed by them. But the disease nearly killed us all,' the old rabbit said, tears in his eyes as he remembered his dead wife.

'Well then, friends,' said Iggy. 'Do we agree to seek an Animal Truce?'

He smiled as he saw all the rabbits nod their heads.

11

The Council of Animals

Four of farmer McCafferty's Friesian cows stared into the big field from the shelter of their shed. The field was covered in snow but now very little of it could be seen. The noise from the thousands of animals standing there rose into the frosty, moonlit sky. Barks, squeals, squeaks, snuffles, and miaows all flowed together into one great sound. It was five minutes to twelve and the second great Council of Animals in the history of that part of the world was about to begin.

In the middle of the stadium-sized field stood a platform made from sticks and branches. It had been constructed an hour earlier by the rats. Standing on the platform was Jeremy, with one of the Wise mice, two wolfhounds, Shane the Great Dane, Ginger and Tom, the twin Persians, Iggy, and the biggest black rat in the whole country. This rat was nearly as big as Barry. He had several wounds on his sleek body and Jeremy shivered as he stood beside him. The rat's name was Nat. With a frightened yelp, Jeremy suddenly recognised the tomcat. Tom was the cat in his dream!

The village clock struck twelve. Now all the animals were hushed. Nat stood up on his hind legs and held up a black paw. He spoke in a high-pitched voice which reached all the animals.

'It has been agreed by the other members of the council

that I am to be their spokes-animal. I will begin by welcoming you all to this historic meeting of the Council of Animals. You are all aware of the Animal Truce and you are bound to obey it. The truce will last for one day after we rescue our friends and the Black Building has been destroyed. And we *will* destroy that terrible place. We *have* to. We cannot allow the humans to test any more animals. Most of you know what goes on in the Black Building but,' he said turning to Jeremy, 'I will let Jeremy mouse tell you what he has seen there.' His bulging eyes stared at Jeremy. Trembling, Jeremy moved to the front of the platform and, with tears in his eyes, told the animals what he had seen.

'There are rooms in the Black Building,' he began. 'Huge rooms with caged dogs . . . ' As he said 'dogs' all the dogs began to growl. 'Caged cats . . . ' All the cats began to tear at the ground with their claws and screech loudly. 'Caged rats . . . ' As he said 'rats' the rats, including Nat, stood on their hind legs and squealed angrily. 'Caged rabbits . . . ' As he said, 'rabbits' all the rabbits and hares, including Iggy, began to thump their hind legs hard against the ground. 'And caged mice . . . ' Now all the mice began to squeak angrily. 'And,' Jeremy shouted, 'they are all suffering. Even as I speak some will have already died. The cruel humans have used our friends and companions as testers for their shampoo and make-up.'

Jeremy sighed heavily and sniffed. 'I've seen rats whose tails had fallen off and were lying in the cage with them. I've seen young pups with sores all over their bodies, crying with pain. I've seen cats with one eye and one ear. The cruel humans are causing these terrible things, just to make sure that the shampoo and make-up which humans use is harmless. Galopocus, the wisest mouse in the land, told me that the humans who work in the Black Building have gone away for their Christmas holidays. He says that now is the time to rescue the prisoners. He told me he will show us how to destroy the Black Building . . . . '

'But how will we get inside?' shouted a long, grey rat.

'We do not have a plan,' said Nat, shuffling beside Jeremy. 'But what we want to know now is, are you all with us? Are you all ready to go to the Black Building and rescue our friends and destroy the horrible place?'

There was silence for a few seconds. Then the field erupted with the sound of all the animals shouting, 'Yessss!'

The shouts went on for a full minute until Nat held up his paw again. 'Follow us,' he shouted. 'And be very quiet. We do not want the humans to see us. Come now, follow us.'

In thirty seconds, the leaders — Nat, the Wise One, the wolfhounds, Shane, Iggy, Tom and the Persians, and Jeremy — were hurrying to the bottom of the field, followed by thousands of other animals.

12
Rescue

The moon rose high in the sky and lit up the huge Black Building. Away at the far end of it, near the security gate, a Doberman barked uneasily. Three other guard dogs sniffed at the frosty air. One of them frowned as he looked at his companions.

'Do you smell anything?' he snarled.

The other Dobermans stretched their necks and sniffed. 'I smell mice,' one of them said.

'No, it's cats . . . I smell cats,' growled the other dog, sniffing.

The first dog growled, 'You're both wrong. It's rabbits. I smell rabbits.'

'Rabbits?' one of the other two snarled. 'It's mice, definitely mice. That cheeky little mouse must have returned.'

'Cats!' snapped the third dog. 'It's cats. Can't you smell them?'

The three guard dogs frowned as they sniffed together. Their bulging eyes widened as the smells of cats, rabbits, rats, mice and dogs came to them in the wind. Then they heard the low noise.

'What is that?' snarled the first of five more guard dogs who came running up to them.

'The fence!' the biggest Doberman snarled. 'Let's get to the fence quickly.'

When they reached the fence they spread out, five

metres apart. The eight dogs glared through the fence at the big chestnut tree on the other side.

Then Jeremy came running out from behind the tree. Growling, the dogs closed in. Their white teeth glistened as they glared at the tiny mouse.

'I'm back again,' said Jeremy, smiling cheekily.

The guard dogs growled again and two of them began to bark loudly as Nat and Barry came out from behind the tree to join Jeremy.

'Let us in,' growled Barry, pressing his nose right up against the wire fence.

Above them Jeremy saw several bats, hovering, watching what was going on.

'Open the gate and let us in,' growled Barry.

The Dobermans looked at each other, astonished at Barry's request.

Suddenly the biggest guard dog came jumping right up to the fence. With his teeth bared, he pressed his face against Barry's and snarled, 'No one can get in while we are on patrol.' He squinted at Barry's crossed eyes. 'Why do you want to get in anyway? This is no place for you or your rodent companions.'

'We want to get in to rescue our friends who are caged inside the Black Building,' Barry studied the big Doberman. 'You must know there are many of our kind suffering in there.'

The Doberman glared at Barry. 'Yes, we know,' he snapped. 'But they are of no concern to us. We have nice cushy jobs here, guarding the building. We are well fed and we don't have to work hard. If we were to let you in to rescue the other animals we could lose our jobs. No, you cannot come in.'

Barry sniffed and moved back from the fence. 'Very well then,' he said, and with that he let out three low barks.

Immediately, from out of the undergrowth came the rest of the dogs. Over one thousand of them gathered, growling, along the fence. They all glared at the fearful guard dogs.

'Now, will you let us in?' growled Barry.

The Dobermans looked at each other.

'I asked you to let us in,' snarled Barry. 'Are you going to?'

'But . . . but there is a human guarding the gate. We can't turn on him. We would lose our jobs if we did that,' whined the big Doberman.

Barry frowned. 'Is there only one human guarding the gate?'

'Yes,' said the guard dog.

Then Nat asked, 'Do you know how the gate opens?'

'No,' lied the Doberman.

'I do,' said the smallest guard dog. 'I've seen the human press the red button. The red button opens the gate.' He smiled.

The other guard dogs glared at him.

'Good . . . good,' said Nat. Then turning to Barry and the other dogs he said, 'I have a plan. But the Dobermans will have to help.'

Barry glared at the guard dogs. 'Are you going to help us?'

The big guard dogs looked hesitant.

'You'll be sorry if you don't,' growled one of the big Irish wolfhounds, moving closer to the fence. 'We'll get in with or without your help. It will be better for you if it is *with* your help.'

The leader of the Dobermans sighed heavily, then growled as he looked at the other guard dogs. 'We'll have to help them.' The seven other dogs nodded.

'Then come closer,' said Nat, 'and listen. This is what I want you to do . . . '

As the dogs discussed the plan, Jeremy looked up at the hovering bats and shouted, 'Please tell Dracula's mother that Jeremy needs his help.'

One minute later Dracula's mother landed on a tree branch above Jeremy. The little mouse told her what he wanted.

Very soon about five hundred bats could be seen flying above the fence towards the roof of the Black Building. Each bat carried a frightened mouse by the tail!

Fifteen seconds after they landed, the mice, led by Jeremy, were dropping down the chimney. When all of them had reached the office Jeremy whispered, 'Follow me.' Hundreds of tiny footprints dotted the carpet as the mice headed for the corridor.

When they had squeezed under the first door their eyes widened at the horror of the caged rabbits.

'We've come to free you,' shouted Jeremy. 'The dogs will be here soon to break down the door.'

'Dogs!' squealed a tiny rabbit.

'Don't worry,' smiled Jeremy. 'An Animal Truce has been called. The dogs will not harm you.'

The mice swarmed around the cages and in a few seconds each cage was opened. Soon all the rabbits were free.

'Stay here until the dogs come,' shouted Jeremy. Then he called to his companions, 'Follow me.'

They went streaming under the next door.

The rats' eyes widened when they saw the mice.

'We have come to rescue you,' shouted Jeremy. 'An Animal Truce has been called. The dogs will be here soon to break down the door. In the meantime we will try to open your cages.'

The rats squealed happily as the tiny mice crowded

around each of the cages. It took a little longer to open these cages, but eventually all the rats were free.

'Now to free the cats,' shouted Jeremy. At this, his companions stared at him. They were afraid. Jeremy smiled. 'They will not harm you when they know about the Animal Truce.'

So the mice went running into the room of cats.

The cats spat and clawed at the mice but they stopped when Jeremy shouted, 'We are here to free you. An Animal Truce has been called. You cannot harm us. The dogs will be here soon to break down the door. In the meantime, allow us to work on opening your cages . . . . '

Meanwhile, Joe Connors, security guard, awoke with a start. He had been dozing in his warm security hut just inside the main gate. He was a young, fair-haired man with a blue security guard's uniform.

'Aoooooohhhh . . . . '

The cry of the Doberman made him stand up and look through the window. Pressing his face against the glass, he looked to his right and saw one of the dogs lying crying in the snow near the gate. Joe looked at the gate. It was locked. He looked all around outside. There was no one about except the dogs. He looked at the red light above the button. Everything seemed fine. The dog howled again.

'I wonder what's wrong with it?' Joe said aloud, reaching for his flashlight. Before opening the door he looked out through the window again. The other dogs were nowhere to be seen. 'Good,' he said. He had had a narrow escape when he had first started his job. It had taken one of the older security guards to save him from a Doberman who had failed to recognise his scent.

The dog howled again. Taking a look towards the

Black Building, Joe opened the door and went outside. He shivered.

As he neared the Doberman, the huge dog rose to its feet. Joe's eyes widened when he saw that the dog was not hurt. He turned to run back to the hut. Sweat broke out on his pale face as three other guard dogs came running from behind the hut. They surrounded him. Trembling, he stood still.

'Easy there, boys,' he croaked, trying to keep the fear from his voice. 'Easy now.' He turned his head slowly to see how far he had to run to get back to the hut. It was then that he saw another Doberman standing on its hind legs and pushing with its nose at the gate button. He gasped as he saw the gate slowly open. He gasped louder when thousands of mice, cats, dogs, rats, and rabbits surged, cheering, through the open gate and on towards the Black Building. When all the animals were inside, the guard dogs began to growl and move towards him. Swinging at them with his flashlight Joe let out a roar to try to frighten them. When they backed away he turned and ran. He could see the other Doberman coming out of the hut, so he ran for the open gate. The dogs watched as he stumbled screaming up the road. Then they turned and ran to join the other animals at the Black Building.

By this time Jeremy and his army had reached the room of mice. They surrounded Galopocus's cage and soon the wise old mouse was free. Jeremy watched as Galopocus crawled from the cage. 'He looks much weaker,' Jeremy said to himself, going to help him.

'Are you all right, Galopocus? The dogs will be here soon to break down the door. Then all the animals will be free. The council called for an Animal Truce.'

Galopocus smiled. 'Your mother?'

'Barry helped us to free her. She is fine now,' said Jeremy, smiling. 'But what about you? You are weak.'

'A little,' said Galopocus, looking around the room at the other mice. 'I'll be OK once I get out of here,' he said. 'When everyone is free, and outside, you and Barry must help me destroy this place.'

Just then the door crashed open and three Great Danes, a St Bernard and two wolfhounds led the other dogs and animals into the room.

'Hurrahhh,' squeaked the mice. 'We're saved . . . We're saved. Hurrahhh . . . '

The big dogs dashed past them and on up to the other door. They threw themselves violently at it. The door burst open after a few tries and the loud barks of the pups could be heard welcoming them.

Now all the animals were hurrying from the Black Building. The sick ones were being helped out by their friends. Soon only Barry boxer, Jeremy, and Galopocus remained.

'Come with me,' said Galopocus. 'I will show you how to destroy this place.'

Outside, the thousands of cheering, excited animals stood around the Black Building. They were waiting to see it being destroyed.

Barry and Jeremy followed Galopocus down three rows of concrete steps. Galopocus seemed to be growing stronger.

'There,' he said stopping at a narrow door which had the words *Fuel Store* written above it. 'Turn the door knob, Barry.'

Barry frowned at the old mouse but, stretching his strong neck, he hit hard on the door knob and turned it. The door opened and the three animals pushed inside.

Outside, a tiny rabbit asked, 'Why is the Black Building not being destroyed?'

'Give them time,' snapped another rabbit. 'The terrible place will soon be destroyed.'

'What now?' asked Jeremy, staring around the room.

'There,' said Galopocus, shuffling across the cold, stone floor to a big, round tank with the word *Oil* written on it. Turning round, he squinted at a red can. 'Do you think you could carry that can over to the tank, Barry? To that tap there?'

Jeremy looked with pride at his big friend as the boxer easily lifted the can and carried it over to the dripping tap on the end of the tank.

'Now, Barry,' said Galopocus, nudging the can into place below the tap. 'Could you grip that tap and turn it on? It might have a bad taste, but do you think you can do it?'

'I'll try,' said Barry.

'There isn't much time to waste, Barry. There is no telling how long it will be before the humans come. We must hurry.'

Stretching his neck, Barry gripped the tap. 'Ughhh,' he spat as he tasted the foul oil. Then, taking a deep breath, he gripped the tap and turned it on quite easily. The oil ran into the can.

When it was nearly full Galopocus said, 'Turn it off now.'

Obediently, Barry did as he was told.

'Good, good. Now for the difficult part of the plan. Barry, do you think you could lift that can of oil and carry it upstairs without spilling it?'

'Yes,' said Barry quietly. 'I believe I could do that.'

'Then follow me,' said Galopocus.

'They're certainly taking their time,' growled Shane to Nat. 'Do you think we should go back inside and see if they're all right? They might need our help.'

'No,' said Nat, his black eyes staring at the entrance to the Black Building. 'Let's give them five minutes.'

Barry carried the can up the stairs and along the corridor to the office where Jeremy had first entered the Black Building. By the time he got there, he was breathing hard because the smell of oil wafting up his nose was making his head light.

'Now,' said Galopocus, pointing to the middle of the floor. 'Put the can down there and knock it over.'

'Knock it over?' said Barry, surprised, as he put the can down.

'Yes, knock it over,' repeated Galopocus.

With a quick look at Jeremy, Barry put his paw on the can and heaved. The three animals jumped back as the oil spilled out of the can and all over the carpeted floor.

'Now,' said Galopocus. 'We have five more trips to make to the oil tank. Do you think you can make it, Barry?' He smiled at the dog.

'Yes,' Barry said, smiling back at him. 'I can make it.'

'Good, then bring the can with you,' said Galopocus.

'What's happening in there?' said Marjorie to herself outside. 'Oh, I do hope Jeremy is not hurt.'

As if reading her mind, one of her friends nuzzled her nose, saying, 'Don't worry. Your brother is very brave. He'll be fine. With Galopocus and the boxer he'll be safe. It shouldn't be long now before we see them coming out again.'

In the last room Barry overturned the sixth can of oil. As the oil spread, Galopocus and Jeremy dragged an oil-soaked cloth from the puddle of oil, down through the rooms, out into the corridor, and into the office. Soon all the puddles of oil were joined together. In the office Galopocus scuttled to an electric fire that lay under the desk. It was plugged in.

'Barry, do you see those books on the desk?'

'Yes.'

'Could you reach them and bring them over to where the electric fire is plugged in?'

'I think so,' said Barry and went to the desk. Standing on his hind legs he grunted with pain as he reached out and nudged the two thick books, off the table, onto the floor. Then he bent and picked them up one at a time and carried them over to Galopocus.

'Place them one on top of the other beside the plug . . . there, good,' said Galopocus. 'One on top of the other, yes, that's it. Good . . . good.'

Barry and Jeremy wondered what Galopocus was up to. They stared as they saw him climb up onto the books and sit down beside the electric plug.

'Now, Barry,' said Galopocus. 'I want you to tip over the electric fire.'

'Tip it over?' said Barry, glancing quickly at Jeremy.

'Yes. Make sure the bars of the fire are facing down into the oily carpet.'

Using his nose, Barry pushed the fire over and Galopocus smiled. He saw that everything was ready.

'Now you both must get out of here,' he said.

'Get out of here? But aren't you coming with us, Galopocus?'

'Yes, in a while. There is something I have to do first. But you two must go.'

Jeremy looked at a puzzled Barry.

'Hurry!' shouted Galopocus suddenly. 'The humans might come anytime. Go! Go!'

'The five minutes are up long ago, Nat,' said Shane. 'I really think we should go inside and see what is keeping them.'

'Yes,' said Nat, thoughtfully. 'Maybe you're right. There must be something wrong, to . . . '

Suddenly there was a great cheer as Jeremy and Barry came running out of the Black Building. They ran straight to Nat and Shane.

'Where's the old mouse?' asked Shane, looking at the building.

'He told us to go,' said Jeremy. 'He said he had one more thing to do.'

Inside, Galopocus reached up with his two front paws and pulled on the switch for the third time. He grunted as he pulled, but then fell back, breathing heavily. 'It's no use,' he cried. 'I'm not strong enough. I'm just not strong enough . . . but I have to destroy this place. I just have to. I cannot allow any more animals to suffer here.' Taking a deep breath, he stood again and stretched his paws up to the switch. Gripping it tightly, he pulled, leaning the full weight of his body on it.

Suddenly with a sharp click it fell into place. Galopocus was caught unawares, and fell, rolling off the books onto the floor. He lay there dazed as the bars on the electric fire grew redder and redder.

'What's keeping him?' whispered Jeremy to Barry.

'I don't know,' the big dog answered, his eyes widening as he saw the flames. 'Look!'

Through the windows of the Black Building they saw the flames licking into the air. More flames shot up into view from another room.

Galopocus awoke, coughing. He saw that he could not reach the door. Flames were roaring all around it. He was trapped. He rose unsteadily to his feet, almost choking as the smoke swirled towards him. Looking around him he saw there was no way out and he prepared to die. 'At least,' he cried as he lay down, 'the Black Building will be destroyed.'

The smoke cleared for a few seconds as the desk caught fire and Galopocus saw the fireplace. 'There *is* a way out!' he exclaimed, rising quickly to his feet.

Dodging around the burning desk, he stumbled, still coughing, to the fireplace. In a few seconds he was inside the chimney and began the long climb to the roof.

Now the whole bottom floor of the Black Building was ablaze and the animals smiled happily as they saw it burn.

Jeremy had tears in his eyes and he kept looking at the doorway of the burning building. The flames were rushing out from it. 'Galopocus must be dead,' he thought sadly.

Smiling, Barry looked at Jeremy. 'Well, Jeremy, that's the end of the Black Building. Maybe the humans will think twice about building another terrible place like that.'

'Yes,' sniffed Jeremy. 'But it cost Galopocus his life.'

'He would have been proud to know he has destroyed the Black Building,' said Barry, turning to look back at the burning building as some of the animals cheered.

'Yes,' said Jeremy slowly. 'I suppose so.'

Galopocus looked up and, as the smoke swirled past him, he could see the starry sky. 'Only a little way to go,' he cried. Taking a deep breath which almost made him choke, he scrambled on up. But by now the flames were being drawn up the chimney and the old mouse could feel his skin beginning to singe. Very frightened, he dug his feet into the soot-covered red brick and, with one great effort that made his head throb harder, he reached the top. Leaping onto the melting snow on the roof he rolled over and over, down towards the spouting. As he did, a funnel of flame erupted like a volcano from the chimney, blasting it apart. The flames roared out of the opening while Galopocus ran along the edge of the spouting towards the down spout. 'I'll be safe if I reach it,' he exclaimed. But below, the building was collapsing.

Jeremy and the other animals jumped out of the way as some bricks and rubble fell to the ground beside them. Backing further away from the burning building, they stared up.

Suddenly Marjorie screamed. 'Look! Oh, Jeremy, look!'

The animals stared up into the black smoke. Jeremy saw Galopocus making his way along the edge of the spouting to the corner of the building.

Suddenly, above Galopocus, some bricks from the chimney began to slide down the wet slates. Galopocus was just in time to jump out of the way as they slid onto the spouting, bringing it crashing down to the ground.

'Galopocus!' screamed Jeremy.

'He's trapped,' whispered Barry as a huge part of the roof collapsed behind the old wise mouse.

As it did, several young mice began to cry. Others turned away, unable to look at the terrible scene.

Now the whole of the inside of the building collapsed. Helpless, the animals could only stare up as Galopocus teetered on the edge of the building that was left standing. It was only a matter of seconds before it too would collapse. Below, the timbers crackled as they burned. Black smoke billowed into the sky.

Jeremy tilted his head and listened. He looked at Barry. The big boxer was listening too, his ears pointed straight up.

'What is it?' whispered Jeremy.

'I don't . . . bells,' gasped Barry. 'It's . . . . '

Suddenly they heard a voice.

'Prancer . . . Dancer. Donner and Blitzen . . . whoa! Rudolph . . . Whoa!'

'Who . . . who is it?' gasped Marjorie. All the animals stared. A human, a white-bearded man, dressed in a red suit and riding on a sleigh pulled by six reindeer, stopped beside Galopocus. With a loud voice he shouted: 'Jump! Jump on board, little mouse!'

Now the animals saw Galopocus jump from the edge of the building, just as it began to sag and crumble on top of the rest of the burning building.

'Galopocus!' screamed Jeremy.

'Don't worry, Jeremy,' shouted the old mouse who had landed safely on the sleigh, 'I am safe now. Goodbye! Perhaps I will see you later. Goodbye!'

As the sleigh rode across the sky the sound of Christmas bells tinkled above the countryside and all the animals smiled.

'Who was *that*?' asked a tiny rabbit, his big eyes bright and glistening.

'The humans call him Santa Claus,' answered an old rat, adding, 'Until now I never believed such a person existed.'

'Santa Claus,' whispered Jeremy, in wonder, as he looked at Barry. It was then that they heard the sound of more bells, fire engine bells.

In seconds the animals were scattering for the fields.

As they headed home Jeremy thought about all that had happened. 'I hope the Animal Truce lasts much longer,' he said to Barry.

They were passing the fisherman's shelter along the river when the town hall clock chimed. It was one hour into Christmas day.

'Happy Christmas, Jeremy,' said Marjorie, smiling.

'Happy Christmas, Marjorie,' Jeremy whispered back.

Later, when they arrived home and all the family had squeezed inside, they were surprised and happy to see that their mother was out of bed. Around her bed lay several huge boxes, tied with ribbons and covered with bright, shiny paper. Two of the boxes were open.

'Look!' cried Marjorie, darting forward and lifting a huge piece of cheese out of one of the boxes.

'And look at this!' gasped Jeremy, tearing the paper from another box to reveal a loaf of bread.

'But . . . but where did all this food come from, mother?' asked Marjorie, watching as her brothers and sisters began to open the other boxes.

'I don't know,' answered her mother. 'I was sleeping and I had a strange dream. I dreamt that the humans' Santa and our wise Galopocus brought in some boxes. When I awoke there they were!'

'But there's enough food here to last us out the winter!' exclaimed Mr Bills, with tears of happiness in his eyes.

Jeremy lived for many Christmasses, until he was a very old wise mouse; in fact he became the wisest mouse in the land. But he would never forget his first adventure or that happy Christmas day.